The Man Who Ate M

and other works

Colin Tan

- Obituary of an autobiography
- Your garden
- She used to cry
- farwell photography
- the puddle.

The Man Who Ate My Arms

he took them
these arms I made strong
from my scrawny childhood
these arms I was saving
to hold my daughter with
these arms I worked with
bled with
and fought with

we all live in the basement
I hear it is nice in the penthouse
I heard it is so
from a media mouse
say the wrong word
act the wrong way
and you can go lower than the basement
on any given day

in the dungeon I was tortured
sliced and diced and boshed and brainwashed
and then he took off my arms
with a smile and a knife and I watched for days
now less of a man as my right and my left
as the right and the left
were marinated and grilled
and he licked his lips, thrilled

I watched him feast and devour
and savour my flavour
the strength I struggled for
the scars I earned through war
he did feast
the horrible beast
and washed me down with a wine
the name of which
I was not allowed to learn
with no privileges to dine
with

I was flung back to the basement
older, weaker and less of a man
but things have improved
we are told now
we have a TV
and every day I have to see
the monster who ate me for tea
and my stomach churns
my shoulder stumps burn
and I vomit in denial and disgust
as if in manufactured lust
it was I who ate my own arms
and this is the reminder
this technological divider
that my arms put him there
right there

The Lady In The Woods

I once was lost in a forest of
willows at the age of thirteen,
after a whole day of drifting
in the mist of green,
I was as tired as adolescence.

The mist cleared and I found myself,
in a glade
and I found the glittering,
the glittering body of a woman.
As dead as the stone she was stuck to
and strung out like a sacrifice.

Fairer than the posters on my wall
and more complete than any movie
I fell asleep to dream in.
Had I witnessed the Myth of Sisyphus?
I could not say but the breeze whispered
"she has essence yet exist, she does not."

I fell asleep with my head at her feet
and my hand on her thigh,
colder than the stone against my back.

I dreamt of her and that glade
every night of every year,
every year the darkness and fear,
of never seeing her again.
I went mad in that forest and
went madder still looking for
my way back again,
every night
of every year.

At last I did with blistered hands
and pieces of a heart.
She glittered brighter,
brighter than the reflection of

the moon on the silver grass
breathing beneath my feet.
"She has essence yet exist, she does not"
whispered the breeze.
And then I heard a laughter,
flutter through the trees.

I turned and she was gone,
"I exist, I exist"
I called to the breeze but that too,
was done.

I could not escape that glade,
my arms were frail and covered
in leaves that drank my tears.
I had become the weeping willow,
after all these nights and years.

Untitled

A man with no name
addresses himself
in sounds and feelings
and recalls visions
and bleeds in colour.
A man with no name
writes in symbols
and moves with music.
A man with no name
does not understand
or need a label.
A world full of labels
has little need of stories.

I Lost My Shadow In An Alley

I went there, where
concrete grows thicker
than trees
and neon lights float
like fruit
without branches.

Imaginings complete a view
without the 4k of the sun,
and with no vanishing
point in this scene,
I had to sacrifice for
perspective.

In the morning I was blind,
without my shadow,
I could not see where
the sun did shine.

"mmmmmmmmmmmm"

mass
medias
mind
marauding
malignancy
makes
meek
morons
morose,
malevolent,
moribund.

An Ode To Something

The sunlight makes me bleed
and I dissolve like milk condensed,
as you stare on blinded
with your pupils peeling like dry onion skin.
This is what it means to be here-
in THIS place,
with sound shattering glass underneath your feet.
We cannot sleep and we cannot wake
and we are trapped in the space between their eyes,
here with no meaning,
but we think and we are they tell us.
Yet, that brings little comfort
to the melted and the blind
whose dreams drank the seas of salt,
for we know not if they are, let alone who they are.
The meaning of who is a what and a where that ends in a why.
Why? Why? Why?
I beseech myself yet have never known myself,
I called out to you because I wanted you;
because you were the only thing,
that I could see in this space.
This is what it means to be here.
This is what I think feeling is,
yet I have never felt a thought
or imagined I was ever real.

I Am The Weatherman

the shake of thunder
and the beat of wonder
the rattles of your chattels
and the flash of electric
a light epileptic
the patter of rain in the gutter
a march of ants in flutter
the sun in the morning as life is yawning
the yellow of beginning to the pink purples of endings
it is enough to say nothing
there is nothing to say
it is not enough to say something
but sufficient to close my eyes and think
of my true dew you
and the words we could say
in silence
as the world comes to play
in violence
and I would care not
if we forgot
to hide inside with eyes fear wide
if you were here to share the dare we have to care
I miss you because I want you
yet we share no tether
and I just want you here
to watch the weather

I Forgot

I forgot my name,
it was not what I chose.
I forgot my religion,
I was not made by a god.
I forgot my mind
by believing my heart
was something stolen.
I forgot my freedom
by being cursed of flesh.
I dream of ideals
but am enslaved by impulse.
I think this is a thought
but know not for sure.
The mind is an idea,
that perpetuates itself,
beyond the self,
until there is no,
self.
I remember.
I forgot.

A Man Is Many Things

a man is many things
when he opens a door
when he holds a hand
when he closes the door
when he lets go the hand
when he cooks something
when he eats something
when he writes
and does not read
when he reads
and does not write
when he knows he is a woman
when he needs a man
when he needs a woman
and then loses her
when he makes music
when he smashes a guitar
when he gives answers
without asking questions
when he follows
and dreams of being a leader
when he leads
and never wanted to
when he does not remind himself
that one day he will not be here
or anywhere

yes
a man is many many things
but
he is truly nothing
when he is made to believe it so

Scrabble

Bauhaus blitzkrieg Beethoven bombs burn brighter
than the tales told to the telephony telemetry clergy,
cajoled conned contained,
clandestine congressions, cryptic confessions, kool-aid
concessions.
Waiting women want worlds within whilst
moping men manipulate moods, moments minutely,
pettily preening paltry passions.
Orgasms organising objectives only,
teeny tiny toys taken to town.
Create escape debate elevate abrogate checkmate.

Chains

The chains around your ankles,
rattle along the road,
like the ringing of the bells you heard in nightmares.
He hung himself from a door,
not the ceiling,
it was easier on the neck that way.
It was easier than the CPR attempt,
on a body that had been lifeless for twelve hours.
Half a day in any time zone,
is long enough time for,
anyone to be gone.
Two months of dates,
conversations,
and one argument rolled into a kiss,
and wasted in a single breath.
This is how it looks, after death.
Outside the courthouse I wait,
reading a book,
in a car,
in the rain.
Knowing full well that inside,
you won't be able to leave the pain.
The coroner, a foreigner,
in the land of your memory.
And the one you will never let go of,
is the moment you were never there,
but was he,
ever really there?

I Imagined

I imagined a life,
very different from my own.
A world where,
the rain quenched my thirst
and food filled more than a hole,
my soul.
Where the sky does not lie,
the blue is true
and you,
hold my hand like I am real.
This is what we all,
want to feel.
Even the rocks that stand alone
are nothing without the earth.
In time the tide of the inside,
will turn that hand to sand.
But for now,
I will dig deep in this brow,
and imagine,
a world of compassion,
until I get home,
having convinced myself,
we are not alone.

Barbarella in Japanese

She is up there on the podium
in a silver two piece of
shimmer and glimmer,
wearing Barbarella,
with Japanese subtitles.
She sways and swings and
floats as they gloat.
The hungry little dogs in the dark corners
and the hyenas on the dance floor who,
all forgot how to speak.
When she glided up there,
when she sidled up there,
like a leaf that stole a magnet
and grew taller than a tree.
There is no mist but smoke
in this little concrete chip jungle.
Just bass and lasers to let
them find their way to urinate,
instead of scents for their noses,
their bladders full and minds empty.
There is only one wolf in the room
and they are as rabbits in her headlights.
As she shines,
she dines,
and all around are ancient.

Awake

I dreamt I was awake,
wide,
wide,
awake.
But I lay in a position
that I never,
ever,
take.
Flat on my back,
staring at the ceiling,
devoid of all feeling.
Then an alarm sounds in the distance,
and I roll over in that instance,
and assume the position,
of which I dreamt.
This is not what life meant,
this is what it means to dream.

Matchstick Girl

The itching begins.
Needles under the skin
remind me that I can't be in it.
I cannot bear myself because
I cannot express myself.
I must escape,
myself.
I cut my skin
to see if that would ease,
if that would release,
me.
But bleeding does not make me feel alive.
It just shows me what is inside,
and I hate that too.
If could set fire to my blood just once,
if I could see it burn just once,
it might prove I have a soul.
And that this body,
that they scorned,
that they cut before I cut,
that they choked and broke,
just might contain something more,
more than I am.
And there might have been a point to all this.

Know This

Know this,
that you are here,
in this moment.
You are alive.
Tears do not come freely,
hold them,
dearly,
and cherish the blemish
that they leave on your soul.
It started out as a blank,
empty,
canvas,
and now these blemishes
are splashes of colour.
Your scars,
the scratch art of your heart,
talk to your fingers.
The sensation lingers
to remind you,
you are here.
Your tears are salted,
exalted with flavour.
Tasteless is lifeless,
you will find no nourishment
on an empty plate.
Know this now,
as I stand here in awe of you,
that I gaze upon a masterpiece,
and I am grateful now,
for the moments that came,
before.
For they led me here,
to the wonder of you.

Lemon

With onyx hair and ruby lips,
she holds out a lemon,
a replacement for the sun
she cannot see,
in this dark room of candlelight.
Slowly, carefully, she remembers
and recalls,
and as she does, she squeezes,
progressively, profoundly.
No juice or tartness stains her hands,
the fruit is dry.
Instead tears form in her eyes
and begin to build and creep,
with every recollection and squeeze.
Tidy hands and a tidy mind,
are a blessing.
I sit and watch from a dark corner,
and sip on gin and cucumber.
She leaves after the candle melts,
and I depart when I place my
empty glass on the floor.
I am afraid that I might slip on
the lemon peel,
in this darkness.

Crumbs

There is a trail of crumbs on the table,
as abrasive under my palms
as the stones under my feet.
A delight in pain I meet,
with some surprise.
The bread of lies from the flour of sighs,
always cleaned my plate.

In this hall of empty chairs and broken stairs,
the only sound to be found is the beat of an eardrum,
a constant thrum that mimics the shape of the crumb,
that I now flick towards the floor.
I never wanted more,
just an open door
and a way out of here and this castle of fear that,
I opened my eye to, breathed my nigh to and sang my cry to.

This place is an orphanage,
a shrine to the pilgrimage
of a journey I did not imagine,
a way I will never fathom.
There are holes in the roof
and stars in the sky and one day I hope to try,
to fly and find them,
with this empty stomach,
I have no weight to keep me on the ground.

Freedom

The struggle towards civil liberty
begins with the struggle for freedom of the mind.
For a mind free from the herds,
from capital gain,
from the institutions,
from the religions,
from the party lines,
from the medias,
from the online,
from the offline,
and from the noise.
Humanity is innate.
The noise is deafening,
it is so loud you cannot hear yourself think,
so you don't try to anymore.

Interlude

The ground is bare and baseless
like an empty matchbox,
the tinder has departed
and there will be,
no,
spark.

I look to the sky and remember birds with wings
and the lips of a lover,
cold in the morning.

If rain were,
now,
to fall upon my head to
deliver doubt desperation,
fear foreboding frustration,
my feet will keep walking.

Rain dries eventually,
but lies,
lies laboriously linger,
acidic and prolific.
My skin burns with a veridic desire,
a digression from my similitude.
I am.
I am,
a man,
on fire.

Revel in the freeform.
Unwind in the undefined
and forget your initial feelings.
There is no meaning in,
no leaning in,
a jerk of the knees,
a conditioned,
disease.

I love to breathe,
air like this,
under a blue moon,
on a path I imagine.
Life appears to be the moments,
I hold in my lungs,
and the space between,
my dreams.
You open your eyes and the interlude,
begins.

Neon In The Bloodstream

there is neon in the bloodstream
this level of substance abuse
is constant and relentless
a glowing omnipresence
plastic pink and proton purple
UFO green and cool cyan
surround the lie of safety yellow

there is no safety in yellow here
raindrops pirouette in the gutter
and your heart will flutter
a beat in the street of sign cloud
that float as high as the skirts on the girls
who smile as bright as the neon twirls
of the straw in the glass
made of a plastic past

you read of love in books but find only
empty fucks
and no hacks in the bar snacks
just the scents of grilled meat, fat and smoke
in electronic vapour you choke

you can dream if you have time to sleep
but the neon light of night will haunt your days
a hangover becomes a layover until
you can be there again
called there again
now that your heart is a battery
of lithium

Another Love Poem

Cold as a winter morning you felt,
the first time my hand stroked
your shining form.
Tears dripped into my palms
as you felt my warmth.
I could sense your heart,
yearning for summer days
and all this pressure,
you bravely held down,
since the day you came to be,
memories of bubbles screaming to burst.

I did not hesitate,
I did not waver,
to emancipate and savour,
all that you had ready for me.
I worked under your lips and
pulled your soul free,
and I drank and I drank
of all that you gave to me.
To the very last drop,
to the bare bitter end
and then tossed you aside
my momentary friend.
I bid you farewell,
in a beat and a tear,
the pain,
anguish,
and loss,
of you,
my last,
can of beer.

a DEATH of sorts

delicate dancers diligently debut

                                                   (dying,

disdained, devoid)

                enter emaciated eunuchs excited

    (explore, evolve, end)

                                       arrows attack and

abate

                            (anger, angst, apathy)

trials test terra's transcendence

                         (toxic, tactless, tired)

                                how humanity's

harangue happens

      (honourless, hatred, harassment)

DEATH

A Drinking Problem

"I think you have a drink problem" she said. A steel glance burned from her blue eyes like stars under the curtain of night, her hair vast and infinite.

"I think you're right, two hands and only one mouth."

"I'm serious."

"I've never had a problem with it before and nobody has a problem getting drunk with me, so it's all good."

"I'm worried about you" her hand pushed my palm against the bar, as she

pushed my body down on to the bed that afternoon.

"It helps to numb the pain."

"The pain of what?"

"Knowing the future."

"Knowing what future?"

"Knowing that you'll leave me."

On Mass

It is folly to assume,
that a body of mass has by implication or necessity,
substance.
A body of mass increases its mass,
to have more weight to chuck around,
to effect agency and causality,
but that is also folly.
Agency is a causality of mass,
but mass has no real agency,
without substance.
Substance of itself is borne from the weight of words and actions,
which by implication can be immeasurable,
and are devoid of any mass.
Hence it is therefore so,
that a thin body of mass that possesses substance,
of itself for itself or another,
can tip the scales of life in its favour.
And a body of mass will always lose,
to a body of substance,
when the true measure of the body is perceived.

A Body

A body is nothing more,
than a home for flesh and bone,
but a home is where you are and choose to be,
in this body or in another,
in this place or in a lover.
Why do you let it weigh you down so?
Why does it dictate where to go? When to say no?
Its nicks and scars,
its position and pattern,
show me only things that happened,
but they do not show anything true,
they do not show me,
you.
Inside is just your mind
and what you imagine and you design.
Take not the instruction of these things,
follow not the template of the desolate,
show me what I see,
behind the hair,
the skin and eyes,
beyond the lips and hips you hide.
What I see is what I feel,
what I want is what you do.
This is the only promise I can seal,
in this place between me and you.
To break free of this flesh and bone,
is the path to the feeling called,
home.

Ghost Ships

At midnight,
the sea is as black as blood,
and all its denizens have
departed from perception.
Here I tread upon this beach,
the sand stained by a million ashtrays,
the dust of wasted discussions
and pointless protestations.
Twenty black shapes emerge from the fog,
and strand upon the beach,
directionless,
leaderless,
and full,
of emptiness.
Vessels of rusted hulls and algae glass,
receptacles of broken dreams and days gone past.
I peer into everyone
and find no one,
not even skeletons,
of men,
but fragments of whale bones instead,
chiming in the wind.
I would leave this place,
but I cannot swim,
and all are stranded here.

The Fall

I drift into freefall
with neither a parachute nor an umbrella
and offer a mango to the winter
but it is bitter and no better than the batter
on the fish we do not eat with chips
I managed a head stand under a waterfall
and that is how the freefall
started

blood
gravity
reality
thud

loved
vanity
insanity
flood

I try to keep warm under a blanket of surrealism
but that institution does not welcome the likes of I
winter is coming and I will be a virgin before spring
this year has gone on too long
we remember the fall but can never recall
if we ever really stood
at all

The Brain Eats

the brain eats
what the mind defeats
and the heart is not smart
enough to think for itself
itself in a state of constant flood
as you drown in your own blood
the pitter patter of grey matter
is a troublesome thing
and the look in her eyes is a disguise
touch her to make her sing
you are not here so have no fear
unless they saw you
unless the saw you
and then you cannot hide in non-existence
behold
your brain will feast upon this sustenance
you will only ever feel alive
when you do not know what is happening
when
you do not know
what is happening

The Girl At The End Of

The world forgot her.
A dress of eggshells
and a collection of shit,
gathered and spread upon the lawn.
The pretence of a canine
a defense of sublime.
Her poetry cannot rhyme,
anymore.
Pulled hair cannot grow
and blistered hands cannot sow.
Her only crime was pubic
an ideal all cherubic.
Razors are for legs not veins,
bleeding hearts beat only blame.
Alas.
Alas.
Why do women bleed?
They ask and ask no further.
The floorboards,
creak of nightmares
and only dust keeps them quiet.
Her house of mirrored walls and empty halls,
was built by many,
and their jibes of confetti.
Scattered at the illusions
she was taught to believe,
and told to conceive.
For so it was wrote,
so she was smote,
she must conceive,
this body,
the mind doth deceive.
The mind,
doth deceive.
The body and a lady,
doth bleed.

The Bandaged Tree

when the sun rose in the east
its leaves would turn to the west
moss would grow on its right
but the trunk would lean to the left

light, night air and rain
screamed, shouted its name and pain
roots deep in soil seep

they tied its trunk
they tied its branches
but from seed to tree
there is only one way it can be
from seed to tree
just like you
and me

The Drugs

the drugs the drugs the drugs
they deliver delectably
empathy or erections
emotions in chemicals
humanity in reactions
no spirituality here
just the realisation
that there is no
spirituality
and that stardust
is nothing more than elements
letters on periodic tables
like the labels
we bestow upon ourselves

from

right

to left

to up

to

down

from white

to

brown

A Late Night

I bleed dreams
like tears under a waterfall.
Mist in the darkness yet we don't understand them.
Ripples flutter in me,
I feel them outside and so the room
is full of pond weed.
Sticklebacks dart above and
whisper away through the mirror.
Why can't they stay?
Fools are lost like sand in wind.
These dreams only come at night.
She left like candle wax,
but it was I who melted.
Metaphor dictates and simile rises against.
The paper calls but not the images.
Smiles from a girl on the way home
are remembered through the rain on
the bus window.

Where am I?

A Stroll

The sky is bubble wrap
pop, pop, pop you go.
Fading into footsteps,
feet tapping concrete
like fingers on piano keys
playing jazz that you only pretend,
to hear.
Breathing smoke,
mortality in every breath,
one more step along parallel lines,
with only a finite number of notes
on this fretboard.
Are you playing your tune,
or somebody else's?
Only time will tell,
when the song ends.
The rain will fall again and again,
taking another half a millimetre
of this city away.
Again
and again,
and again.
Try and catch a sunset now and then.
seek the place where the light sleeps,
rest not where the sky weeps,
onto the soil where they sow the dead to grow.
Another bubble bursts and
pop, pop, pop goes the sky.

A Dream of Orion

Orion has no shoulders,
and the world is weightless, floating, spinning
like the mind of one in love.
Yet we bear its weight on our shoulders
and succumb to a gravity and not a levity.
These thoughts came to me,
as I trod barefoot in the pastures of my mind,
through dreams that linger as does tobacco scent,
but do not grow as does the plant.
I wish for whispers in the shadows of leaves
and beckonings in the glimmers of summer rain,
but these things do not appear and I tend to disappear.
In the middle of a glade in my mind,
a shadow and fade I find,
of who I used to imagine I was.
Thoughts are precarious and have a tendency to
become delirious when the notion of a heart is involved.
But we cannot witness the machinations of a heart or mind,
through the empty vessels of the heart and brain,
these notions are not the same.
Ideas and souls are formless
yet without them we are gormless.
If there is a nobility in this solitary profundity,
then I can depart this battered shell in glee and dignity,
but therein lies the irony,
I will not be here to witness the finale,
a thin fin et al.

And Animals Are As

and animals are as
pompous prickly people promoting peremptory politics
insipid insects inciting incriminating immunity
fly far for freedom fly far from flies
that try to take the truth
away and act as animals are as
beasts biological brainless bumbling buffoons
technology transplants terminates the triumvirate
of man woman and child
of memory will and wild
how to survive
how to be alive
when the noise steals your ears
and screens steal your eyes
the noise screams your fears
the screens create your lies
act as animals are and
feed ferociously
forsake fealty

A Righting Life

Chasing these words,
desperately digging them out
from under my veins
with this rusty blade
these fucking things
that crawl under my skin
constantly,
chasing
constantly,
tormented.
A little booze slows them down
and you catch a few,
a little too much
and they leave you for a while,
more empty than before,
because the drink is a
trap,
too.
Some memories a constant itch,
like the scratching of an overdose.
Some dreams so vivid
that when they leave you,
they leave you.
Blind.
Where is the nobility in chasing ink?
Where is the nobility in chasing drink?
Stop pretending.
There are no heroes to be found,
in blank pages and empty glasses.
Stop pretending.
There is no suffering for
your art.
But look
and look again
and find art in suffering,
and when you do
you must not stop.
You will give too much
for far too little

because empathy is not easy
and neither is trying to be alive,
and knowing where we are,
and knowing we are here.

Suburbia

This house is over two hundred and thirty years old,
nobody lives here and nobody ever really did.
The roof beams still rattle in terror with the memory of the sound
of the crack of the leather belt
and the screams that hammered the walls.
The lonely bathroom now colder than ever,
contains a mirror that still sees
the boy who had the reflection of a girl,
and her tears that fell into the sink
and were lost in the running water
that she used to drown her sadness.
The floorboards still have the
desperate creak from the feet,
of another girl who would sneak,
away to the first one who gave her attention.
And to freedom from the sermon and derogation,
from the mother who had been alone since impregnation.
A mother who believed Jesus would
give her attention.
The girl snuck out to a lonely labour also,
and her mother SCREAMED it was a punishment.
The bedroom curtains yearn to be opened to the sun,
to forget the man who could not afford insulin.
The rest of the world did,
long,
before he passed.
The jungle of weeds outside,
rejoice since Julio got deported.
Remember Julio,
Julio had a name.
They sing taller and louder than
the opium poppies,
that pulsed through the veins and tears,
of the other girl who needed them
to drown out the sound
of the knock on her bedroom door.
The knock that shook her bones
day after day year after year

until she could hear,
no more.
Never enough money entered this
house from any corporation or entity,
and always too much was sucked away
by many a material deity.
They built this house on blood-soaked land
and have stolen from it ever since.
This house is over two hundred and thirty years old,
nobody lives here,
and nobody ever really did.

This house is America.

Whales

I heard whale songs in the bedroom
as I lay hump backed and prone
pathetic and alone
I guess that is how it seemed
in this drowning dream
stranded
beached
impeached by own mind
no quarter can I find
in the corners of this room
there is nothing solid
about a place
or construct
that you know you will leave
at some point you perceive
all rooms are temporal
all bodies are made of paper
except those we cannot see
those we take with us
wherever we may be
from room to body to mind
from places to faces and kind
carousels of confinement
revel in our fragility
the loan of our humanity
that we often squander
before sinking
like whales who cannot sing
I would drown in the rain
were it not for these windows
I turn to see the shape of a face in the pillows
and discover that I left this place
with the minnows and morrows

Good Morning

Good Morning,
my friend.
Your life has been dawning,
since the first moment you screamed
and you forgot to breathe.
Your death has been yawning,
apathetic, lethargic, a litany of monotony,
waiting and abating, hungrily, impatiently.
The idea of your heart beats a mourning,
the opening of your eyes begins the lies
and the morning brings a warning.
Take heed my friend,
take need my friend,
from the moments, the whispers,
the air in your ears and the words in your lungs.
Take heed my friend,
concede my friend,
that not all questions have answers,
not all moments are chances,
breathe your words do not speak them,
close your eyes and see them.
This,
is a warning,
fear not the yawning,
live not the mourning,
you can always choose,
coffee, or booze.

Visits

The crying of a tortured beast,
plagued by inner demons
echoing out from dark caves.
Passes out onto a cold, wet beach,
whispering waves on the shore,
like the tired cries of lost souls.

Departure in a rocket.

Wind chimes bounce through the air,
butterflies flutter under chirping birds.
Drops slide down green, smooth rocks,
into the infinite pool,
at the base of a waterfall.
All around there is jade, emerald green.
Everything coated in fresh dew.
An old thin man,
behind a long grey beard,
sits dripping wet,
blowing into a flute,
which is really a mandolin,
or so it sounds.
Everywhere the chime of nature's chorus.
Moss, moss, how are you today,
you sticky thing.

Departure in a rocket.
Shooting, flaming stones.
Patter like hail stones in rain,
down onto battered copper pans,
of sound and sand.
Around the deep sonorous murmur,
of a hollow organism,
somewhere.
Yet, I hear a sorrowful lead guitar.
Again the murmur.
Perhaps a beep too,
sorrow at the wasted desolation.

Stand and see the song view, sound scene.
And cast your tears down like Moon Whales,
humpbacked and pathetic.

Departure in a rocket.

The World At The End Of The Bar

Conversations travel,
from election to war,
across the sea and back in time.
Tears of laughter,
tales of crime.
Moments flicker in each word,
as do splashes from a brush,
the canvas a smile,
a grimace,
a tear,
or blush.
The heat in the glass,
passes through my veins with each beat.
And each time it fades,
I look for one I cannot meet
The whole world is at the end of the bar,
but I'm stuck in my glass,
sinking in pools of you,
until the glass and my world,
is empty,
too.

Acting Classes

She took acting classes
but could never cry at funerals,
as empty as the boxes
they put in the ground,
feelings,
nowhere,
to be found.
Eyes as dry as the lies,
she told herself to be alive.
Her arteries,
alleyways,
clogged.
Dead ends of wires
and forgotten wrappers,
like torn up love letters
that comforted not the heart
but the stomach
that churned.
The acid that burned,
like the tears she never learned,
to make to fake to take
and water the flowers,
she had to pretend to smell.
She could not be taught how to,
feel,
and could not remember being,
born,
and won't remember the day she,
will die.

And neither will I.
Neither will,
I.

Storey By Story

It is beautiful up here.
The buildings morph into one
like a forest at night,
painted with a splash
of Christmas lights.
The shimmer in the windows
sparkles in the dark.
And I am in awe as the breeze
sucks my breath away,
like the stars did the sun.

I take off my jacket,
fold it neatly like
an origami swan
and place it squarely on the ledge.
Next,
my grey woollen socks
and brown leather shoes.
I tuck the socks into them,
like my mother use to tuck me
and place the shoes on my jacket,
like the flowers on her grave.

This is where I was.

The ledge under my feet
reminds me of that stony beach,
where.
I cut my foot on broken glass.
I bled then and I was alive,
the sand soaked it up so fast that
I never got to know how red it was.

I lean forward with one foot pointing downwards
as if I am about to sink into a cold pool.
Before I realise I'm off,
I am flying or falling,
feathers,

and leaves are twins in the wind.

The same breeze that took my
breath away now fills my cheeks
and ruffles them like a hair dryer,
my lips shaking with the violent kisses.

I feel the air between my toes
for the first time in my life.
In endings there are always beginnings.

Don't look down they say
so I try to look up,
but I cannot with this pull.
The best I can do is look straight ahead
and see the windows fly by,
each one a picture frame.

They're watching the news,
even now I can't avoid the ginger cunt.
This guy throws his dinner against the wall,
it explodes like a firework of
china, beef and gravy.
This kid's stuck in front of the TV,
alone
the place is empty.
I remember being on the sofa like that,
sinking in blankets and cushions with someone.
She's cooking,
but she does not wear a hungry face.
Why are you on the treadmill at this time?
You shouldn't run in the dark.
That flower on the windowsill
does not miss the daylight
and neither do I.

Wait.
She saw me.
Wait.
She sees me.

I manage to turn my head slightly
like a drunken man in bed,
and squint as the wind tries to close my eyes.

The look on her face.
Wait.
That look on her face.
Wait.
I'm not ready.

THUD CRACKLE BURST.

My mind tries to call out
for the ends of my fingers and toes
but they are either not there
or neither am I.
I am not sure what I am,
looking at,
there is fluid filling up behind my eyes,
like a tide calling out to me.
They are right,
you know.
Your life does flash
before your eyes.

Writing Is Like Lego

love is apportioned in raindrops
and sunlight teases laughter
there are only
three nice days a year
and the weatherman
is a con man
they keep asking me to write more
find more
be more
but most days
smiles come together like Lego
and that is what writing is

good meals finally came
when I cooked for myself
and so
I write for myself
and occasionally somebody else
but to be read is a dream
to be seen
to be seen
amongst all the raindrops
that fall from lonely clouds

Whispers

There is a reflection in your eyes
a dereliction of a constitution,
polished black pools that reflect more
than I ever wished to see.
The truth.

Bleed red and talk in blue
this is what I did to you.
Bleed red and talk in blue,
this is what I mean to you.

There's a fire on the streets
so bright it burnt the moon, pink.
We got off the bus at the end of the world
and laughed as we watched it head back again.
We thought we made it.

Bleed red and talk in blue
in the gutters and corners.
Live dead and die in truth
all your sons and daughters.

The whispers I heard on the windows
teased me like the raindrops
I used to need
to drown out the sound in my head.

Bleed away your tears and talk in songs.
Drowning in sound is where we belong.
The choke and the cough of your wrongs,
a rhythm and beat of the forgotten strong.

Trickles of currents
leave our minds
like the memories
of lives that nobody witnessed.
That birds never sang for
and the wind never called for,

that the trees did not grow for,
this life that you,
did not ask for.

Animals

bleeding is a dark art
there are no dreams in genes
no ideals in helices
there is no biology
in humanity
this planet is a zoo
we are born into cages
and fed to fear the freedom
in the absurd

Titanium

Tap dancing on a titanium floor
avoiding eye contact and smiles
as a rhythm takes me to the future
I love electricity, gorging on buzz
there's a guy on a drum machine
shadow boxing on plastic pads
and a skinny girl splashed in PVC
whispering into a microphone
she's so loud
she jiggles my bones
and wriggles, my clothes
ohhhh I'm shuddering like a mother suffering
I have a rule, principles are im-portent
if the colour of my drink
is not bright enough to see when I close my eyes
I will not drink that glow, you know
I will stay until they throw me out
I will stay until she hears me out
there is nothing outside anyway
there
      never
           was
I never was
           here
                could be
      anywhere but
there

The Scream

Listen.

I can't take it anymore.
The drone of the traffic,
the horns and the noise,
the bad manners and the stammers,
of logic and reason.
The thud of the window only dulls
it to a hum.
And my heart throbs,
like a blocked pipe,
clogged.

The shit you talk about,
is as interesting as the kid in the street,
dishing out credit card applications,
like a charity.
You're no less a vampire
and less of a machination,
my sweet.
It's not the kids' fault,
they gave him no choice,
but you,
you don't wanna choose.
anything.

Listen.

Peace is silence or noise beyond a scream.
If you want that space to be empty.

Don't let them in.
Fill it.

What God Said To Man

Tears.
Dreams of blood that was never pumped,
from a heart you never had.
You saw with your ears,
and listened with your eyes.
Learned nothing, oh learn-ed one.
Pain.
Pleasure.
Gifts unwrapped and unappreciated.
A child of random design,
I am.
Your poetry is all the same.
Words,
as meaningless as your existence.
And therein lies the rub.
Is there really salt in your tears?

The Eye of the I

In the eye of the I and the tooth in the tooth,
there is nothing to forsake, forsooth the truth.
At midnight, every night,
she wails and wails her screams a gale, her tears, a veil.
The gown as black as the frown on the priest who passed her the
news,
this truly terrible exchange of views.
Views are the news that the ear is inclined to hear,
when the cock forgets to sing,
when the sky the sun forgets to bring,
and the children pull the butterflys wings.
Her wails rattle the beams so loud and profound,
leaves on the trees outside shudder to the ground.
She was made in seven days
and in another seven days
she will be no more.
She was loved in seven ways
and in another seven ways
she will love,
no more.
She swallowed this book and choked on this book,
of binding for no finding,
just the eye in the I and the tooth in the tooth,
with nothing to forsake,
forsooth the truth.

The End Of The World

The ground is not flat,
there is a wibble in my left,
and a wobble in my right.
I open my mouth and speak purple,
this is not a song to sing,
feet,
do not mean anything.
They never did when I wore shoes.
My eyes see beyond the end of the street
to end of the world.
If I could steady my legs,
long enough to pluck petals from a rose,
long enough for the bars to close,
I might have something to smell,
a scent to follow in the next life.
A trail of tears, a mist of melancholic meaning,
a grail of fears, the gist of alcoholic seeming.
Pray prudently poor parents,
life lies, love loses,
hearts hear hate horizontally,
desires delude despair diametrically.
It's been the end of the world for a time,
it was never a beginning.
With each breath you steal you choke a little more,
and the one word you ask for,
is the one you could not say,
yesterday.

Heroes

This guy speaks to me.
He talks my language.
The language I was taught to speak.
The language I want to hear.
He is clever.
He points out the flaws,
in what you say and do.
He says what should be happening,
and does nothing.
He talks of a destination,
and makes no journey.
His voice soothes,
when yours hits a nerve.
He is a hero,
through and through.
I can't hear you brother.
I don't get what you say.
I don't like the sound of your voice.
But this clever guy I like.
He,
is sharp.
He,
talks my language.
The language from schools,
comic books and movies,
spoken in the little leagues and the ivy leagues,
binary and divisory.
He helps me forget,
what I was taught to forget,
that heroes are not supposed,
to make me feel comfortable.

Ice Cream for Breakfast

I fell as far as my eyelids closed,
as far as the sun rose,
or my childhood hand from the ice cream,
or the space between you and me in this,
recurring dream.

I hate to dream of you.
The barbed hand of night
creeps up from nowhere,
up through the mattress,
into my flesh and tangles,
around my heart and twists,
and drags it down to nothing.
until I wake in the mourning,
tired,
exhausted,
and adrift on this ocean of a bed.

Photos On The Wall

without the photos on the wall
she would have forgotten
all the meals she shared
the spice the salt and the sweet
the beer the wine and the water
on the lips of the kisses and promises
sunrise above the ocean and tangled bodies on the sand
legs betwixt legs heart to heart and hand in hand
the shivers in the snow and balls she did throw
the joy the sheer joy of being raised on shoulders
in a sea of people as music rained in boulders
a wall, an entire wall and another and a floor and a ceiling
of minutes moments memories meandering mostly ghoslty
now
her lifetime would fill this place and then some
but will flash play in seconds the moment she is gone
the beer was flat
and wet was the mat
as it dripped on my rice
as useless a device
as the photos on the wall
I studied and searched amongst them all
but in the end I too lost this game
and therein could not find my name

Pyramid Hill

They called it pyramid hill
because of its shape,
although it had been there for almost as long
longer than anybody could remember
not my father,
my father's father, or great grandfathers' father or even farther,
back.

They all remember her,
they have seen her
at least once in their lives.
The hair so black,
it shines with stars,
the skin so pure it reflects the moon.
The eyes that see beyond,
you,
and more,
forever more.

They say she drove men mad,
because of this and these
because she did not do as they pleased.
They tied her to a pole
cut from the wood of seven trees,
at the top of the pyramid hill,
the point,
fixed towards the moon,
grey gloom in bloom.

They poured black tar,
gathered from near and far,
from her head to her feet,
but it seemed as though
her hair fell down to meet,
the earth.

They tried to set her alight
for every single night

of the following week and month.
Yet she did not burn,
and they came to learn
that their scorn could not remove her,
their fire could not harm her
and eventually
the town retreated from the hill,
and people stay away still.

I had never known love
and I had never seen beauty,
but I dreamed of both once
and awoke in duty,
to discover that and more.

I took a pen and paper
and a bottle of whisky for the journey
and set out to find myself and
the true meaning of beauty.
The stars called out to me
and the moon cried tears for me,
until I found myself
at the bottom of the hill,
my heart and the air,
completely still.

The moon was directly above the summit
as I climbed and I did find
her, tied to the black wood.
Bound with grey cord so tight,
with excessive might that her skin,
bulged beyond its undulations.
Tied across her mouth and cherry lips,
her wrists and ocean hips,
pulled back as far as the tide.

Those eyes,
those eyes,
both tired and awake,
called out to me to take,

the cord from her mouth,
and unsheathe her teeth,
tombstones of diamonds,
refractions of the enlightened.

"What is your name?"
her voice asked from behind my eyes.
I could not even try to reply,
the words that formed were lies.
I had finally,
uncovered their disguise.

Spilled Milk

Before you lies a dead body.
Stiff, cold and prone,
sprawled across the floor in front of you.
The eyes as opaque as those of a stale fish.
The skin tone,
hard to place,
somewhere between yellow and grey.
Inside that head were thoughts once,
that mouth spoke words once.
Close your eyes,
and imagine them.
You have seen it somewhere before,
somewhere other than your floor,
beyond your hand,
your phone,
and your home.
This is not a game,
I need to know its name.
Are we not all,
the same?

Nosferatu at Noon

The sunlight hammers my balcony
to a time of thirty four degrees
At four PM
it is bleached and burns Sahara song.

I.

A Nosferatu at noon
dare not take my chances,
in need of blood
and merry dances.
At night I will drink a beer there
or pass a joint of my arm,
and let my mind put the jigsaw together,
of the light splashes,
charmed.

At noon
I chanced it once
Nosferatu I
I read Borges and was bored so,
that my sweat reminded me of greater needs,
and fears.
Fear of those who would see my face
the pale fruit afraid of the sun
and those with fingers to point
"mat saleh", "ang mor", "gweilo"
for they know not what I am.
Yet at noon I would devour them for lunch,
if they ever speak of Borges,
this Nosferatu,

I.

Palace

My heart became an empty hall
and my flesh and bone a withered palace around it.
Where the memories I have of us,
slowly come to worship the empty
space and fade away,
one by one,
the ashes of prayers for your return.
But prayers are never answered.
and palaces always decay in solitude.

Paper Cuts

Paper cuts slice deep and clean,
they sting longer than your tears run
but never leave a scar.
Give me those paper cuts
any day of the week,
the ones I earned in faraway lands
and running through passages and paragraphs.
Give me those paper cuts rather
than the words you sliced and
diced me with,
than the words you beat me down with
deeper than the shit your dog dumps,
that stick to my soul like a tattoo I never
wanted and have to read every day
to remind myself of how shit you make the world.
Scars that grow,
The more attention they get.
Give me those paper cuts I earned escaping myself,
those paper cuts that taught me to express myself.
Give me those paper cuts and I'll
bleed all over your precious fucking floor
and drown you in who
I am.

The Obituary Of An Autobiography

I swore I wouldn't kill anyone
because I wanted to be a novelist
I wanted to relish each and every moment
of my tiny existence
and find something worth writing about
something human
my desire to be human was such
that I pretended to love
that I pretended to be a child
that I pretended to be a man
and tried to imagine pain
in the end
I found nothing but
empty pages and hollow words
paper cages and empty worlds
in the end
in the end
I had no choice
but to kill you
my little darlings
and toss paper away
again and again
how prolific I have become
in the murder, torture and death
of the self
just to put my life
on a bookshelf

[Handwritten annotations:]

I did the opposite with my crime thriller

Not understanding who we are = quintessential human

the roles we play

super wordplay!

right images, gentle verbs (delicate act)

suet! brutality in contrast

Do we create roles for ourselves:
'the husband'
'the lover'
'the manager'
'the client'
'the carer'
just to hide from the fear that we have NO CLUE who we really are.
The artist gets over this fear, to search for meaning - but it's PAINFUL

Art is pain

Bukowski - my poems are tiny crumpled scrapped on the floor of my cage

Today

pools on black concrete
from twilight rain
hold reflections of the city
fragments of above that we only see
when we look down
streetlights are beautiful in ripples
as are lips when they flutter
smiles caught in reflections
that you find from people behind
are the brightest
we all want to be wanted
we all want to get wet
we need the puddles
to catch the light
and sometimes the reflections
of who we are
but we always complain about the rain
only the brave look up in a storm
and only the blind look into the sun
we think we see too much
but we do not see enough
look closer
look further
there is an ocean in every puddle
a river in every gutter
and a heartbeat
in every flutter
of your lips
on
mine
your tears
the raindrops
on
mine
empty the clouds from your head
before you are dead
my friend
today is

today is
today is
the only day you are alive

The Wind Stole My Memories

The wind stole my memories,
there was no contest and no way to protest,
pervasive and inescapable, it is.
All around and everywhere, this wind is not, the air.
I inhale and nothing can I smell,
all I perceive is a tickling in my nostrils,
which seems like something that happened in my childhood,
that I can no longer remember.
I assume I was a child once.
I reach out in violence,
and try to take hold of it,
to take it all back,
but I clasp nothing.
And I am reminded,
that I have forgotten how to hold on to something.
I look at these hands,
and I know not what to call them.
I know not my name,
or this shame
that I think I feel.
I am left with shadows and blurs
and words have become slurs.
The wind stole my memories,
after I stole my first breath.
We are not supposed to remember,
anything after our death.

Torii Mountain

So many wish,
to take the same picture and strike the same pose.
So many wish,
to visit the same place and wear the same clothes.
Yet I find myself standing here,
at the base of a mountain and a stony path,
the way above covered by a series of red Torii gates.
There is a pedestal to my right,
where I leave an offering of my watch and my phone.
There is another to my left,
where I leave my pen and my notebook.
I begin my ascent,
with a single deep breath,
and after some time,
I am aware of a view,
in the corner of my eye to the right.
I pause my journey to take a look,
and find myself back at the beginning again.
My offerings are still where I left them,
and so I begin to climb once more.
After some time,
I am aware of a splash of colour,
flowers of many kinds in the corner of my eye to the left.
I pause my journey to take a look,
and find myself at the bottom of the mountain again.
My offerings remain,
now spoiled with morning dew,
it is too late to take them back,
a promise once given must be delivered.
My feet begin to climb again,
I keep my eyes on the path,
and remind myself
that there is a better view,
at the summit of myself.

Empty Room

It is an empty room,
four walls,
a floor,
a ceiling,
sometimes a door.
As big or,
as small
as you imagine.
I do not really care.
There was once a chair,
the type you are visualizing now.
I am visualizing the creases,
on your perplexed brow.
Walls white.
Floor white.
Ceiling white.

Or

did you see,
black walls,
a black floor
a black ceiling,
are you dreaming?
It is only a room
you have been here before.
There may have been a door,
it has been empty forever more.
I can meet you here,
it is quite near,
behind all you seek to find,
behind the eyes that made you blind.
It is only a room,
an empty room,
and this was a poem
about nothing
but an empty room
with no door,
or?

Asthmatic

I love you.
But I don't know you.
Just the idea of you,
is enough.
A whim, a notion
that was planted after I was first born
after the first touch
to have a feeling of my own
is enough.
And the last.
Feelings.
Germinate like seeds
and thoughts,
metamorphose into needs.
And metaphors.
And metaphors.
Open doors
into the little rooms
full of big ideas,
held onto like dyspnnoea.
Close your eyes
and avoid pavement cracks
like a dance routine.
Choke on lies
and slapped backs,
like a wet dream.

Adrift

There are no ripples and no current.
No breeze, or clouds,
the serenity is terrifying.
As I drift amongst the stars,
further away than I ever could imagine, I recall when,
my feet were on the ground.
When my feet were on the ground,
I held your hand once,
your fingers flowed through the valleys of mine.
But nothing flows here,
not even the blood in my brain.
It is now frozen,
like this moment I held onto,
this memory I grasped,
as I breathed my last.
I will now forever be in that moment,
what was left of what made me think,
what was left of what made me drink,
every time I recalled it,
and remembered I lost it.
But now I have reclaimed it,
now and forever,
as my icy husk drifts and sifts
amongst the dust and rust
of Saturn's rings,
with only reflections of the stars
to light up my dead eyes.

Your Garden

You have a garden, somewhere.
At night, the dark is so bright
that you close your eyes.
The shards of grass are frozen,
yet warm your feet.
There is no breeze
except the air from your lungs which
will wax and wane
as the moon does the same.
The moon that rises from behind
your pupils
and escapes not
from those, closed, blind, eyes.
You will spend your whole time there,
watching, waiting, welcoming
a single drop
of something like rain
that will fall in the same spot
again and again and again and again,
as a pool begins to form and your mind
in scorn, will deform.
You will freeze as ripples emerge from
the outside in
and the raindrop will reverse its course
and chase the moon from the surface,
until a larger shape appears
and begins to rise like the lies,
of a creation.
A figure, a form, not unlike your own
will stand on the water
baseless and faceless,
you will see nothing within it.
No eyes to see,
no mouth to speak,
no ears to hear,
and no air to breathe.
This is what awaits
this cruelest of fates

Handwritten annotations:
- So non-committal, indifferent. Nothing special.
- Slow building pressure of impending madness
- are we really here? Most would strongly argue - Yes! Yes! Of course! what if we did the opposite?

at the bottom of your garden,
where the birds have no wings
and the trees do not sing
for you stole the wind
the first time you emerged,
from the pool.

Accept the insanity,
embrace the absurdity.
There is still time.

We so very much
in desire for control.
To embrace absurdity is the
healthiest control. Let go. Do it.
Positive
end.

- Gothically terrifying. The stuff of
nightmares.

- Subverting the rosy warmth of this metaphorical
title 'Your Garden' - a very safe euphemism for
a lovely place - THIS GARDEN IS HELLISH.

- It is the toils and struggles of life,
and yet, here is still time!

Tired

It's numb,
it drags on you like the moments before a car crash,
like the acidic departure of a drug,
nerves in a constant buzz.
At night car lights and fireflies
pulse through grey arteries
and trees are as black as clouds.
An old man sleeps on concrete,
with a book for a pillow
and he dreams of me in another life.
A young boy in purple paisley pyjamas,
needs to read to not dream,
for his dreams are too vivid and too real
and so the days become a blur.
Imagine only being able to see
when your eyes are closed.
The world will become deaf
to anything you say.
Your shadow is your reflection
and your bed is full of noise.
And you wish you had an idea,
a perception,
an image,
to hug.

Handwritten annotations:

what a simile! So many won't have experienced this but it brilliantly conjurs an existential dread.

— there is some magic there but in dead vessels; ergo, hard to find

Solace, in some form; he needs nothing more.

bursts to life with the alliteration and colour — Youth!

} — the artist's curse? Unfiltered to the world's beauty.

Cherry Blossom

The old Japanese lady told me,
when she was young,
everybody was fascinated with America,
but that they also detested it.
I can imagine that,
four people in a room,
sleeping on tatami mats.
Every Friday night just before twelve,
she would try to take pictures of her inner self,
with a camera held in front of the mirror.
When she developed them,
they came out black and white,
always.
After a while she realised that was how they were told,
the world was supposed to look.
So she went out into the city,
to photograph others,
burn scars from bombs,
graves of soldiers long gone,
and people who called the emperor god.
She found guilt, she found shame, and leaders to blame,
but she found no colour,
because there is no colour in war.
"That's only in the movies" she said,
and laughed "but all the flags look pretty."
I poured her some tea, asked her if she wanted milk,
and she laughed again.

The Bar On The Asteroid

I try to visualise the orbit of this place, and I see water, spinning down the plug hole and coming back up again the opposite way. That is all I can say about this place, this place in this rock between Jupiter and Ganymede. I remember plug holes from long ago, before so many of us went into to a deep freeze, and the lucky ones that thawed out were allowed to leave, after being declared virus free. We do not have plug holes now, or wet baths or showers.

Somebody told me about those that were left behind. They drink water, eat meat and grow vegetables but some die of disease. I cannot remember disease, or cheese or meat or my feet on solid ground, up here there's nothing of that sort to be found, and you realise that solid ground, is a myth.

This view though, and real glass, real glass! Nothing beamed through screens or digital paper rolls, this is the real deal. The burning eye is ever watching, set within its diameters of red, orange, amber and fire. The eye of Jupiter always makes me feel that we are not alone out here, there is more that watches our lives than just, the Sun. Perched on this stool of magnesium and titanium, with a cushion of dust I drink the view of the solar system. I cannot remember the name of this turquoise liquid in this steel cup. It tastes of things, memories that my mind is still waiting to defrost. They say that is normal, for those who went under and were frozen and I often wonder who, they, are.

There are sounds to be found in the corners and lines and words and rhymes of this place. One voice says prose and another poetry but the rest I cannot define. There is rhythm and a treble singing, through the Air-Fi. I turn to look inward and feel I have approached myself. There are others here, in this place between a moon and a planet, not unlike any others that you would find in a place between a moon and a planet, I think.

They wear colours that I think are neon and I have a flashback to a city I once loved, where I had someone I once loved. I cannot remember its name or theirs. As I empty my glass, I see that I cannot see very much, are they faceless? Is there not supposed to be more there? In the place between the ears, in this place between a moon and a planet. Perhaps they are too far away or too close for me to see. Perhaps they are too far or to too close for them to be. I raise my hand in front of me, my palm a totem of my existence, and touch my face.

I feel nothing, my fingers enter space and tickle gas a million miles away. I rummage around and cast stars aside like pebbles in an aquarium, or was it called a solarium? I retrieve my hand and observe that there is now something on my palm, the shape of an eye, and I observe that I am being observed yet again. Or am I observing myself, from within? My hand reaches my glass and I observe that it too is empty. Perhaps I drank my face, or my reflection as I watched through the glass. Perhaps they all did, in this place between a moon and a planet.

The Lesson For A Son

love broke this man
as he tried to drown himself
in the water
under her tongue
and then he tried to drown himself
in the pond
under the reeds
under the sound of the crickets
and the trees
bubbling
rumbling
grumbling
like the words he never said
the promise he should have kept
but in the
clutter clatter
mutter matter
of a man who cannot stand
up for what he wants
there is nothing
to be heard
on the wind
or under water
she is a better man's daughter
and he
has forgotten her

Drums

There is a drum beat in the dark,
a bass that rattles the concrete
and shakes your bones.
It is so loud,
it boils the blood in your brain
and rams through your eardrums
like a steam train.
You cannot escape it
it is always with you
in front,
behind,
outside and inside.
It never ends,
your life on repeat.
It never begins
this constant beat.
Close your eyes
and think of nothing,
and you will hear it again and again
thump, thump, thump,
that lump,
the sound of your heart.
Catch it,
seize it
the rhythm of your art.
Nobody breaks it,
you break yourself.
Nobody makes it,
you make yourself.
Bang that drum,
shake that drum,
until you can close your eyes
and not hear it anymore.
Until you can close your eyes
and not fear it anymore.

She Used To Cry

She used to cry,
alone in her room,
just for something to do.
It was kind of like,
an operational check,
to verify systems were functioning,
normally.
Yes,
she had the ability to produce tears.
Yes,
she had the humanity to induce fears.
But in others,
not herself.
Her only fear,
was of herself,
and lack of self,
and lack of fears,
that induced tears,
just the fear that each tear,
was a drop of nothing,
that appeared,
when she had nothing,
to do.
Music was just a vibration,
my touch just a notion,
that she could not imagine.
Her hierarchy of needs was a prison of a prism,
that made each triangle a square,
with no diameter for care.
My arms went around
but there was nothing,
to be found.
I tasted one of the tears once,
to feel one of the fears once,
but could not taste a thing,
no emotion did it bring,
there is no seasoning without meaning.
Like the millions now I wear a mask,

loss of humanity -
- technology
- rigid timetable
all to keep
capilist system
turning.

very interesting use of
'humanity' - is part of humanity
the inherent drive to
harm others?

afraid to lose my sense,
of taste,
and touch,
of haste,
and much.
And the world is fading away,
day after day after yesterday and today
and some,
times,
now,
I really do not know how,
I too cry alone in my room,
for something,
to do.
And she watches from the corner,
now having found something else,
to do.

Tess

calibrating.

- Voyeuristic.

*- Vampyric. To wear
someone down so much
through one's own histrionics
and melodrama, trying to find
meaning through calibrating one's
emotional systems. When someone
tries to bring real meaning, they
break them too as a way of
saying - 'see, it isn't just me
that's fucked!*

*cyclical
heartbreak.*

Flayed Fingers

The Body of Scars

They found him at the foot of the damn of fire,
that they built to keep the flames from the river of books.
These men of non-uniform,
wept at the sight of him,
sobbed at the mess of him.
His arm still in the crack where the damn burst,
the flames had burnt him naked,
and the rain had washed away the soot,
and shimmered across his body of scars,
the tales he carried with him.
The eye of horus shaped tissue,
from a knife in the lower back.
The slashes across each cheek,
and the tear across the forehead.
The punctures towards the kidneys,
and the flesh stripped from his ankle.
How they wept at these reminders,
and grieved for his bones when they cut him from his arm,
to lay a piece of him to rest.
The gnarled knuckles and bent finger,
the ridged skull and raised cheek,
all spoke to them.
They took turns to touch them all,
as if leafing the pages of a book,
and narrated as they shook.
Of the all the flesh he tore,
of all the scars he bore,
the deepest were in his mind,
the most beautiful you could find.

The Centre Is Not In The Middle

The centre is not in the middle and a triangular theorem strengthens squares, rectangles, buildings and bridges. The write hand is not always right and the left is sometimes over there, but often nearby, or over the under hand at the top of the understand, but just to the middle of the misunderstand. A missing of the bullseyes or a mission of lies can lead to a cancellation, yet the centre is not in the middle, it's just cultured that way. Cultivation leads to motivation if germination stems not from circumspection but genuflection and admiration towards the circumnavigation of the middle, through to the centre and the eye of the bull, shit. Mathematics teaches thoughts of logic but a language of expression teaches thought. An ability to express often finds redress in the quite logical fact that the centre, is not necessarily, in the middle but I digress and this poem is your redress that I must diligently, express.

Tell Me

Tell me,
my government does a great job
and the opposition will ruin me.
Tell me,
they are the enemy and are stealing my way of life,
but it is you who take my dreams away.
Tell me,
things are better than ever,
but those in the street live not in the market.
Tell me,
your love is the only thing that is right,
but continue to touch me in ways that are wrong.
Tell me,
I am important and that I matter,
and then tell me what to think.
Tell me,
what you tell me in school,
to keep in line and not be a fool.
Tell me,
in church that your god,
is the one true god amongst a thousand.
Tell me,
that only this planet has life,
among the trillion stars in the sky.
Tell me,
you love me and nobody else,
and do nothing but think of yourself.
Tell me,
you really want to get to know me,
because I tick the empty boxes you were given.
Tell me,
no man is an island,
but everything you do makes this so.
Tell me,
you really love my writing,
but this language is not my creation.
Tell me,
I always have a choice,

but I did not choose to be here.

Coffee Bags

I build mountains of coffee bags,
kopi, keopi and kohi.
Great dams of bitter chocolate beans,
that stem the flow between the valleys,
of the surface of what they call my brain.
She prefers tea bags to Chanel,
and lets her mind flow freely.
Mine is rusty, ground so fine,
I can lose it like dust on a sneeze.
Its been ground for years,
and percolated under high pressure.
It filtered away the fears,
when my heart brought conjecture.
They build higher and higher like a funeral pyre
and at their bottom a bog.
Stale, black tar,
from the drops that were never drank.
It reminds me of people in the street,
being looked down upon by those who can,
from up so high they forgot the sky.
Drops that were never drank,
yet boiled and filtered still,
roasted and toasted without will.
I pour for more,
this chore is a bore.
This cup I drink from,
this goblet I think from,
is an addiction that is allowed,
one you can be proud,
of when you pretend to fit in,
to the din and sin and whim of the world.
To the gay and play and way of the world.
I need something to thump this lump,
of a heart,
a kick start for the art,
of living.
But I find not enough giving,
in the ground little bean,

I am sure somebody somewhere,
out there,
knows what I mean.

Fleas In The Mist

I am in my usual pose,
cheek impaled upon my fist,
complicit in my contemplation.
My ankles flutter limply in the breeze,
as I am perched here upon the end of this steel girder,
it creaks slightly under the crane.
The shadow of it is lost upon me,
and the view of the city below.
When the mist comes,
what few trees I can see disappear,
as if they grew limbs and departed in despair.
The forest was replaced long ago,
and the mist turns the buildings,
into the menacing fingers of a concrete beast,
reaching out from depths I cannot fathom.
I could not have perceived such a vision without this vapour,
a breath of warning in the morning.
Perhaps this time,
when the fog recedes,
I will no longer perceive,
the streets and cars and people below,
but the arms and head of the monster below.
The crane creaks again,
and tells me I have outstayed my welcome,
and so I pick up my feet and dance and skip,
across to the next building, as a flea does from dog to cat.
And the imprint of my fist on my cheek,
tells me that is all we are.

Lunar Cycles

The world lied to me,
when she cried to me,
I thought I was a good man,
a better man,
but I had become,
just a man.
A man of education, effort and dreams,
a fan of morals and conformity not deformity,
it seemed.
But the world became a lie,
when she began to cry,
and I began to die,
when I too began to lie.
To myself to yourself to himself to herself to themselves.
If I am truly canine,
why is not the sun the same colour as the moon?
If I am really deaf why does my heart and pulse hear her tune?
There must be hope at the end of this rope to make loose this noose
that the world unfurled,
a horde of the umbilical cord.
The world in a word in a herd of one,
the hurt in a flirt of none.
Let the tears flow and catch the glow
of the stars that shimmer in them,
and cast back the reflections,
the rumours of Lunar the chromatic consumer.

Variegate this spectrum of a binary urinary
and heed the deed of the seed that was sown and grown
into this monotony of a dichotomy.

Breath

I awoke on a pillow
of black raven feathers
in shock and despair I found myself there
upon them and amongst them
and it was not the case
that I could not catch my breath
I had forgotten how to breathe
my lungs were no longer aware of the air
my mind could not find
its way into the capillaries and ancillaries
that absorb that which we forget we need
like blood when we bleed
I stumble towards the door
the feathers litter my floor
what else did I lose in this dream
what fright in the middle of night
stole my might my will to fight and the light
I needed to see
If I survive this day
what else will be taken away
when I lie on the pillow of feathers
I may dream of my grave
my mind cannot save
me or my soul
for that is how I sank into this hole
I may lose limbs
I may lose senses
perhaps I lost my wings
and shed all these feathers

Paper Boats

Paper boats and muddy coats,
were found on the bank of the river.
Stranded perhaps underhanded,
the last of the little ones decided to leave,
only the old man decided to grieve.
"I don't believe in the ringing of those bells,
I never have, I never will.
I'd rather listen to what the wind tells,
let them free do not kill"
he roared to crowd.
With his last phlegmy cough,
he smiled as he fell off,
the jetty and plunged into the undercurrent,
and held his breath to hunt,
for a sign of life in the groan and foam.
Just as his lungs were about to burst,
from a desire to live without thirst,
he heard voices, nay singing
as the last beats of his heart were ringing.
A little hand clasped his own,
and above the surface he was shown,
the greener grass of the field,
beyond the bells and those who kneeled,
to run with the sun once again,
as a child of light from back then.

[handwritten margin notes:]

This character understands something of the essence of living and isn't afraid to shout it loud. Admirable

— beautiful metaphor for the human experience

saved by child.

liberation = importance of embracing one's inner child.

Life and the act of living. More importantly, why live? What purpose can you find?

Walk With Me

Walk with me.
Fear not to forget me not,
this tour of my mind is the kind,
that will live in you,
for you,
because of you.
For those who have eyes to see,
must read.
And those who have hearts to be,
must bleed.
Walk with me.
You need not be alone on this page.
There is wax on the candles in the corner,
it melts as slow as any moment does,
in the dark.
The sound of your heart mimics the sound
of the souls of your feet
as they try to find the beat,
that your ears want to feel.
Feel.
Feel the air enter your nose,
this is a start,
be aware of the blood,
in your heart.
Walk with me.
Fear not the puddles in these streets,
wet feet will dry in time,
keep walking,
we got time.
Look at that girl,
with diamonds on her ears,
pearls on her neck
and stones in her heart.
Each beat, each pump, each thump
will hurt,
and the only glitter is bitter,
that's no way to live.
Walk with me,

don't leave me alone,
there are stars in the sky you know,
don't ask me how but the moonlight
paints my brow.
This is my mind,
dig deep,
be greedy,
be needy,
I hope you find some kind of kind,
ness.
There is no mess in less,
just the light of a dream from the
dark room we just left.
When the candle burns out,
the smoke will sting your nose,
one day you will have to feel that too,
it's ok to be, you.
Walk with me.
See the lights in this city
there is one and two and colours more than blue,
for me and you and him and her and they,
too.
You do not need rain for rainbows here,
just open eyes to see the lights and sights,
that we all are,
that we all are.
Walk with us.
We're all here,
in every tear,
in every fear,
in every cheer.
We're all here,
bleeding on the floor,
running out the door,
opening our eyes, ears and mouths for,
more,
more,
more.
See the river purple,
the candle wax keeps the paper boats afloat,

think about that as we walk,
read my words as we talk.
Look at him in the garden,
he wears nothing
but he knows how to wear it so well,
you wanted that once,
you wore that,
once.
Keep walking,
you won't remember how you got here,
keep reading with haste,
for this is just a taste
and all this is just the beginning,
it's not time to let go of our hands yet.
Whispers want winter when words wilt without why,
fear forms fanaticism forgoing feelings,
alliterating and abating without creating,
the sounds of those who cannot walk,
and can only talk,
of nothing,
for they dream of nothing,
and feel,
nothing.

I Am Here

I am here
yet he sees me
not
please forget me
not

those eyes
those brown eyes
what do they hide?
what have they seen?
they have never seen me
my reflection
not bright enough
to get behind them

his lips say many things
but a kiss from them
would mean so much more
to wake in the morning
and see his teeth
shine in a smile
like the one crack in the curtains
we always leave
to remind us that we want to wake up again

I know
every speck and fleck
and freckle and speckle
on that face
so well
I could name every one

that one rogue
eyebrow
jousting from beyond
it could tickle my mind into dreams
the faint scar
on his left cheek
that says in braille
"I survived"

I love him so
but he loves me
not
he knows me
not

the closest I get to touching him
is to be above
the dust in the corner
that the broom never catches
that the vacuum never snatches
ashes of him
crumbs of him
pieces of him
tiny
micro
puzzles
of Rosetta
that if I could read
I would know his mind

there is no light bright enough
no spark I can reflect enough
to pierce the deep
behind those eyes
if only I were more than I am
if I were at least
his shadow
I could walk with him
in the sun

If I could
I would
I should
break through this glass
and step out from behind
this mirror he hates himself in
every day
and put my arms
around him
kiss him
and say
it's okay

Travelling

Am I travelling,
when one foot gradually moves
in front of the other?
Am I going places,
if I start at one point and end
at another?
Is there no destination
without a journey?
Or no journey
without a destination?
The road leads the way,
the lines carry me in one direction,
lines I did not paint,
and tarmac I did not lay.
Faces are as raindrops,
in the storm of a crowd,
and the ground appears flat,
yet,
I still trip.
That may not be the case,
if I had a hand to hold,
but then I would be tempted to put
her on my shoulders,
blind her with the sun,
and carry her to where we
cannot see.

Language: The Word Game

There is a constant misunderstanding,
in understanding.
A way of not knowing in knowing.
There is a picture in my mind,
and another in yours.
An insect in a box requires not,
a label.
One should keep these things in a glass bottle,
before one lets them out.
You probably imagined
a different bug to I,
such a rub a dub dub this rub.
I am not talking to Schrödinger,
I stopped chasing the pussy a while back.
Poetry paints pictures, perhaps pink perhaps purple.
People perceive perniciously, promulgating
prerogatives, provoking perspectives, proclamations,
popularising philosophical,
piracy.
Oh.
The irony.

The Random Spring

I have no idea, no recollection,
from whence it came.
No premise can I formulate,
for its existence and its random appearance on the
floor of my lounge.
This silver coiled store of energy,
a guarantee of resistance and cushion of force,
unloaded in my mind.
Formless spirals reaching out for fragments of what came before.
I did not have much to drink,
half a bottle of wine and perhaps four cans of beer
but then I did imagine that
I paid somebody a compliment.
Putting pieces together is difficult in spirals,
segments are not obvious,
perhaps that is why DNA is so.
The food was delicious,
Turkish- meze, lamb, scents of the Bosphorus.
The conversation was fluid as always,
but the spiral appeared without any defined origin.
It was not there when I got home
and it fits nothing
there are no missing components
to anything in this room.
Perhaps it is I
with the components missing
or perhaps I was visited by my clockwork self
and I had a conversation with myself,
and like all good conversations
left behind a piece of myself.
And here I am,
wound up and coiled
with a finite time
and lack of rhyme.
I am looking at it now
and it kind of bothers me,
like the things we want to say and do not say
and the things we want to do and never do.

All this momentum,
compacted,
stored,
imprisoned in steel
with no way out,
just lost going around and around
from upside to down,
like the water down the plug hole,
and I,
this I,
holding on to a soul.

Nothing Has Happened

Nothing has happened
for days, weeks, months and years
no talk, no song, no laughs nor tears
the man on the news
said the world was on fire
I believed he was a liar
so I stayed indoors
with the company of my flaws
and waited unabated
for the nothing
something happened
but I was inside
pretending to be alive
I slowly began to forget
pain, fear, regret
the sound of my voice
how I laugh at a joke
the feeling of food
in my throat as I choke
in the end
I could bear it no longer
the emptiness stronger and stronger
I dialled up the nob
and lit up the hob
the blood red disc
a flag of the sun
I slapped down my palm
and screamed and cried at the harm
that I had done to myself
that I had given to myself
then I passed out of myself
I awoke on the floor and headed out through the door
my hand was on fire
pain is no liar
and out on the street
a crowd of people I did meet
they held up my hand, high to the sky
and screamed loud

and screamed proud
"we've been waiting for you
for days, weeks, months and years,
we've been waiting for your voice,
your laughter and tears."

I Open My Mouth

I open my mouth,
to silence and,
my breath is as crisp, cool, winter air.
The sunlight is behind my eyes.
I was told once,
that's where the light should be,
for any, kind, of picture,
for any, kind, of scripture.
I love flickers, more like stickers, than real pictures,
small enough and portable enough to remember,
with any degree, of self-confidence.
I look at my watch and laugh,
what a waste of time it is,
if you could hear time it would not sound,
tick,
tock.
If you could see time you would not see a clock.
Time sounds like a dial tone,
a constant drone,
divided by the disciples,
the measurers of a change,
that never occurs and whose beliefs,
change,
nothing.
They map out,
years, months, weeks, days and seconds,
these cartographers of calamity,
purveyors of vanity and mortality.
This watch,
is a shackle and chain,
a cackle and drain,
on moments that never get to be memories.
I unclasp my hand and let it fall to the land,
they told me was the ground,
where our species was found.
They tell me,
what love is,
what my name is,

what life is,
this game is,
every time they open their mouths.
I see nothing,
I hear nothing,
I say nothing,
unless,
you see me,
you talk to me,
and you can hear me.
That is what love is,
that is what life is,
that is what this game is,
and this is what happens,
when my mouth opens.
Kiss,
me,
please.

Let Me Bleed

Let me bleed,
as I lay here,
watching my blood tickle the tarmac.
Acidic rain in torrents,
blasts it into the gutter.
The slap of the raindrops on my face,
is the only thing keeping my eyes open.
I'm not the only one lying here,
who can't see the colour of blood anymore.
Let me breathe,
instead of choking me on this water,
that you use to feed the plastic plants,
that you sell to houses in cardboard boxes,
in irony.
A soggy newspaper page,
has moulded itself to the shape of the road,
and it's the best piece of news I've seen all year.
Let me be,
as I try to sleep and hope to dream,
as I try to imagine I am more than I seem.
Let me be,
as try to mould hope like a piece of clay,
as I use clumsy hands to get through the day.
Let me be,
don't tell me I'm not.
Let me be,
don't say you forgot.
Let me be,
I can choose my own name.
Let me be,
why must every day seem the same?
Let me be!
When this rain passes,
I will stand up again.

I Heard A Weeping

I heard a weeping.
as I saw the edge of a cliff.

At the back of my mind.
a phantom sound,
a memory found
in despair,
in this lair
that I built around me
because I never found we,
again.

There is a cave below,
that echoes when the tide is out
and becomes a bubble when the waves return
as your eyes
open
and
close.

I see your voice in leaves that float on the waves,
free from roots they do not sink,
free from roots they do not think,
and give to the fish
dreams of snow,
and wings.

There is no island behind this cliff,
no trees above these seas,
no ground to be found
or earth to meet,
my feet.
My eyes are a street,
that the world crossed too many times.

I imagine many things,
now,
the leaves blossom,

your voice sings.
I try to call out,
hold my breath to shout
but my lungs are a bubble,
the tides is in and this din and this sin,
is silenced.
As the sun closes her eyes
the moon tells his lies,
and the stars pin holes and cry,
in the night sky,
until I,
open
my eyes
and realise,
that there is a distance between my mind,
and my feet.

I Fell

I fell.
My ankle wobbled on a cobble,
but my elbows broke my fall,
and left patches on my jacket,
like those of a teacher man.
Despite being on my knees like a preacher man,
my consternation was the revelation,
that I had been waiting for.
If I could stand upside down,
the clouds would be the ground
and the sky, a town.
I do not drink coffee to wake up,
I drink coffee to make up,
an illusion of having a plan for the day.
And that is when the terror comes,
the anxiety of making plans,
the need for a modicum of purpose,
just enough to justify the opening of my eyes
and to pick away the dream salt left behind by
the tears of imaginings.
I listen to music in my earphones to drown
out the noise in my mind,
the crackle and rattle and static of the erratic.
Thoughts.
Sounds.
Come and go,
pass over, leftovers,
as the lines on my palms multiply,
the days of forgotten dreams pass by,
and leave these scars of missed opportunities.
I had asthma as a child,
and drowned without water.
That is what pressure does to a child,
who sleeps under a pillow to hide.
Yet I am thankful for these strong legs,
they have always granted me levity,
from all this,
gravity.

Mind Palace

From the palace of my mind
I try to imagine more of my kind.
I step out from these paper walls
and linen halls
and sit on my throne of earth to
address this dearth.
I watch the rain bubble along the cobble,
outside on your side to the inside.
I see my city in tears,
these streets once full of feet,
fade year by year,
as fear upon fear,
builds in this mind that does not find,
its way each day
and knows not how to say,
the name of the one I seek.
The eighth day of the week,
that I toil in seven sins for,
a picture I cannot draw,
a remembrance of absence,
a constant, covenant.
There is a war coming,
a clarion drumming,
of heart and mind,
of art and kind.
My palace will burn,
my blood will yearn,
until I learn,
that the kingdom is free,
the glory is we,
and the lie is I.
I am the eye and the ear of the fear and the teeth of the grief and the
lust of the bust that sits in the hall to celebrate the fall that I planned
for myself the day I became a self and dreamt of myself to give a
name to this game and frame my lettered shame.

Selected Haiku

*

forest firmament
finite form follows function
forsaken fears found

*

wet blades bleed rain so
blood cries in mourning, cries pass
streets pulse in crowds, gone

*

sun rises not pay
and the forgotten retrenched
exist, no essence

*

islands deeper than
iceberg people will remain
cities drink the flood

Bottle Glass

The world ended when the bottle emptied,
and I blew a tune like a bassoon,
with my lips across its tip.
Drained, devoid, done.
Dinner, denouement, drunk.
The bottle emptied when the world ended.
I had nothing else to talk about,
and nothing else to smile about,
in this whisper of carelessness.
I imagine ships carrying messages,
across this sea of wine,
only to be trapped in empty bottles.
and broken by bare feet on the beach.
The beach that dogs piss on,
and sandcastles run away from,
with the paw prints they stole in the morning,
just as the wine is pouring.
I want to find warm cockles,
and not empty bottles,
but I feel like a silly cunt,
in this empty treasure hunt.
The metal detector sounds my heartbeat,
and there is glass stuck in my feet,
and there is water water all around, but not a drop to drink.

Wet Wall

I cannot taste the coffee,
my mouth is a congealed swamp.
Each and every heartbeat,
aches in my head,
and my eyes cannot focus.
Seconds pass by,
and I am aware that time
is forever,
running away from me.
I did not want this,
nobody does.
Breathing becomes,
difficult
when you do it consciously,
as do many things.
I watch rain meander down a wall,
it wiggles like worms,
as if alive,
yet the water is only reacting
to the undulations it encounters,
quite often like you and I.
It will disappear when the weather changes,
diligently dancing its delicate denouement.
Earnest expression, ecstatic enthusiasm,
I have not.
Here comes the sun,
sang George,
and songs also end.

This Place

I do not understand this place,
there is a field of glass,
ivy, rust, amber, crimson,
reflections of autumn
in shards of broken bottles.
The wind talks of free will,
but always takes my breath away.
When I try to ask a question,
it begins to hail
and the thunder mocks my vulnerability.
There are images and designs of men,
all around,
at right angles,
perpendiculars
and postulations.
I do not understand this place.
My heartbeat hurts my ears,
I keep imagining the shapes of flowers,
yet find none amongst the grass or at the feet of statues,
just grazes and grit in the palms of my hands.
There is a train that runs on tired tracks,
from one point to the next to the point of the ending.
The carriages are empty,
save for the old man who waits in the aisle seat,
for somebody to talk to.
I heard he tried to set fire to himself once,
in the solitude of winter.
I believe we forgot about spring.
There was never a beginning,
just a sound on the back of my hand,
like the slap of a gnat.
This place,
has a spectrum in the sky,
a disorder of an order that defines.
There are constellations to be found,
of one type and another,
we are all up there,
to be found.

Down.
Here.
A place like this,
this place,
of writings and imagining,
has feelings beyond the tips of my fingers.
Far beyond the sound of my thoughts,
there are marks left on the paper,
shapes and signs that I do not understand.
This place belongs not to I,
for I am not the one reading.
You will see far more than I,
you will see another place,
which I also,
do not understand.

Farewell Photography

They lie on the floor,
a score of women black and white,
mourning in monochrome.
Cracked nails tearing at hair,
legs and arms thrashing on concrete.
They lost shadows in alleys,
and the blurred numbers on keypads,
could not be dialled.
Stray dogs like angry wolves piss on posts,
and the blur of streetlights float like ghosts.
The capture of the rapture occurs,
in the lens of a Leica,
the eyes are spared the nightmare,
of a connection,
there is a safety in refraction,
beyond the hands.
If you listen,
very carefully,
you can hear the raindrops,
taunt the men in the window,
for thinking they knew it all.
Drop by drop they fall,
as will we all,
but not before we say farewell,
to shadows and photographs,
that were never captured.

Handwritten annotations:

lost shadow

- Blade-Runner sci-fi
  bleak.
  Far East (Malaysia)
  - apt image for
    the times

Mindful moment -
here lies the
secret

— in a nutshell, every king,
president, politician in
history -
as important as a single
raindrop in an endless
ocean

C. Dido mur

FUCK NOSTALGIA

→ Very existential- nothing
really matters, nor exists
  ↳ Deliciously bleak.
    → only the now exists -
      so pay attention!

The Church With No Roof

fire burns
and then you learn
my heart catches
the beat of my feet as they meet the street
the ground underneath me
there is nothing above me
come I'll show you
come!
I will show you
up the steps and here we are
the truth is not as far
as you imagined or envisioned

here in this church with no roof
bombed in the war the god was aloof
look up to the sky and see the lie
he was not there he is not there
it is for you to finally care
for the here and now
and not the here, after
for the why and not the how

there are vines on the walls
and weeds on the floor
moss in the hall
and air for the door

the truth is apparent
the city will be reclaimed
you will perish with it in the green flames of blame
I
will climb the walls
and seize
cloud after cloud
until I am as far as the sun

and the truth
will blind your eyes

as I cast down nothing
and show you nothing

there is nothing beyond
but the heartbeat of feet on the street
and girl you were supposed to meet, here
to watch the flowers grow
a tapestry of time to sow
wrap it around yourself
embrace yourself
it is cold in the beyond
the truth burns
and then you learn
how to live beyond lies
and see more than their eyes
the look in her eyes
a reflection

They Float

they float
feet pretending to walk
their heads at ninety degrees
to the sky
searching for a neon sun
but finding only a flicker
an implication
of something within
the constant
drone
dilates
dictates
rhythm
rhyme
revolution
cannot
start
I cannot
be
here
my feet are on the ground
soggy
soaked
squelching in
fear
there are two reasons
why we
avoid eye contact with strangers
we are afraid to see ourselves
or each other
hold out your arm
let the wind take your hand

Paper Flower

a paper flower grows
in a garden of plastic
stem of card
leaves of couche
and pollen of tissue dust
polyvinyl worms burrow the acrylic
feeding feasting fallow
the bees devour the memories of trees
and sell them to the birds beyond the weatherproofing
with pen and hands
I cannot till this earth
so I will fold and unfold
write my contrite
until the flower becomes a tree
and the roots shatter the earth

Curdled

Her words
curdled in his stomach
and he was struck by a nausea.
Reality was once again,
without essence.
The absurdity of his existence,
was at its most prominent,
in solitude.
Only the brave or damaged,
live alone.
We all die,
alone,
we arrive,
alone,
yet constantly fear so,
being.
If there is some place,
from whence we came,
it must be sparce on company,
a sea of I and me.
Perhaps the challenge is to be,
with,
or without,
and not halved,
throughout.
But the sickness in his stomach,
made him realise,
he actually wasn't brave enough,
to believe her love was not a lie.
That she,
was whole,
and he,
just might,
have been able to be,
more,
than half of a man.

The Puddle

From a distance,
the abandoned apartments look like
damaged egg cartons.
Up close you will see blisters of paint,
infected by moss
and dirt that defied the air.
The government built them to provide,
but all they did was hide,
those that the world did not want to see.
I lay here with my head in a pillow of a puddle,
and I often imagine that,
if I could reach out and grab the wire from the ceiling,
from the old light that replaced the sun,
I could pull myself up off the floor.
The cockroach on the wall,
seems to know what I am thinking,
he has waited a year for me to get over the fear,
of using my legs.
This place stinks I think,
but my nose lost the prose,
of fresh air long ago.
I never needed an alarm,
never feared any harm,
when I held onto the
perfect portrait picture,
the tangible treasured tincture,
of you and what you do,
in my mind.
Alas I can no longer find,
or recall or enthral,
myself in your likeness,
anymore.
I know of you,
but cannot see you,
anymore.

I have been here longer than the paint on the walls,
and I am no less thin and this silence is a din,

except for the drip drop drip of the lip,
of the rusty pipe that leaks and almost speaks,
of my shame.

Love saved me,
and its loss ruined me,
and I only lie in this puddle,
to avoid the muddle,
of seeing the blood leave my head,
and this imagined romance,
dead.

light, bouncy rhyme
juxtaposes the
weight
of the
shame

Heartache — Defcon 4

Binge

The man with the eye patch,
took a drag and never exhaled
as he drank coffee from Marfa.
Spanglish wrangled across the table
and Marlboro became a moot point.
Another drag,
and yet another,
and never an exhalation,
just a silent proclamation,
beneath his hat.
A beggar lay on the steps of the obelisk,
a cigarette in hand,
he exhaled,
and exhaled,
as he stared at the left-over burger.
Food,
he could never swallow,
his denial of a tomorrow,
and both of them wondered,
if there was any life outside the television.
Binge. Watch. Repeat.
Binge. Watch. Repeat.
Do not,
do not,
forget to eat.

[Handwritten annotations:]

the eyes worship the box

Two profoundly broken and grizzled characters - addicted. Their "foulness" testifies to the decaying force of a TV diet.

→ they sense their own addiction.

← and yet both have forgotten to breathe. Wonderful!! The unbelievably subversive force of vacuous pursuits.

Manic Mansions

You can find the building in any city.
Jump in the car jump on the train.
Walk,
then pause for breath.
Close your eyes,
turn around and open,
the door that is front of you.

Double oak and aged well,
the rest of it concrete,
black iron and gloom but,
at night emerald, amber and crimson hues,
ember from the windows.

Turn around go up and down,
take your time or run around.
The stairs lead in all directions,
made of Escher and carved of dreams.
The doors are all the same,
green, steel and government regulation scenes.
The rooms inside are yours to find and decide.

The Japanese woman on the ground floor,
makes perfume from roses and bergamot.
Every night before she sleeps,
she reads the fifty-seven letters that her husband sent her,
before he died in fifty-seven seconds,
when he barrelled his plane into a cruiser,
screaming out her name.
Each one of them said the same,
he was too young to die and too old to be a fool,
but man enough to be in love.

On the first floor lives a French man,
tortoise rim spectacles and a twirled, waxed moustache.
He was raised in an orphanage and,
collects busts of stone, clay and ceramic.

Any face or profile that he imagines
could be his father,
fills his place on pedestals,
the foundations of his imagination,
and tears.

On the second floor is the woman.
The woman of curves and jasmine,
whose fingers induce spasms
and linens drown the sons of women.
There is a smoking area somewhere near,
with no windows or ventilation.
Just like the lungs of that cowboy on the poster,
whose horse waits outside,
too free to be inside.

On the third floor are the twins,
who draw on the walls in crayon,
black and blue and gold and green,
squares and circles and flowers and dreams.
Their mattresses are bare but they don't care,
for sleep comes not,
to the forgotten lot,
scorned by the deities of the eighties,
lest we forget, the voters forgot.

The door to the roof is jammed,
but may be opened by the slam of a hand,
of a man with a plan and a fist of a clam,
with a heart for a stand of under,
the wood will shatter asunder.

Up there you will see the cities,
above an oasis of puddles of rain.
The stars in the night will only come out,
when the moon decides to cry,
and in them you can catch,
memories and reflections of the sun.

The Artist In A Space

What is a space?
A distance between two points?
From A to B along one two three,
or the air between you and me?
Perhaps it is the sound at
the end of a conversation,
from one point being made to another,
from brother to brother to a bother,
or to bother,
another.
Perhaps it is that place she
takes herself to when,
she draws solid, smooth lines,
as rapidly as she thinks
and as steady as her words.

My hands have a constant tremor,
a tremble and a fumble,
fingers unable to point,
to a point from A to B along
one, two, three.
Words do not come as easily as lines,
they should never be forced like rhymes,
but the end point is as hard with both.
That is what it is,
finding the point,
the meaning behind all this.
But I always find my way along her lines,
as people do in rhyme from time to time.
Her pictures speak in many words
and my words speak in many images,
and ultimately,
absolutely,
in a way,
we speak the same language.

And that is why I miss her,
her,

in her space as she pours art from her heart
and the page lights up her face.
In that space,
she creates,
in the dark in her dreams,
or on a train awake,
she seems.

A man without his space,
is as lost as a leaf in the wind.
The litter of autumn,
the amnesia of summer,
forgotten and unnoticed,
underfoot.

An artist creates a space,
in any time or place,
regardless of what the world may dictate.
The strife in life and a heart that aches,
will always,
mark,
the spot.

Become,
create,
and find your place,
in your space.
It is here,
beyond your fear.
Nothing more,
nothing less.
Inside is how,
and outside is now.

I thought I had nothing to
write about,
until she asked me to.
And there I was again,
in my space,
and in, our place.

Wine Gums

It was one of those days,
and had been one of those nights.
I got out of bed for a drink.
A bottle opener in the drawer,
and a bottle nowhere to be found.
No cans of beer in the fridge,
and very, little ice.
This was nothing strange,
just an example of my climate change.

It was cold outside,
The condensation on the window,
sniggered at and triggered me and,
took great delight in my plight.
My jacket, like the bottle opener,
was also nowhere,
to be found.

I wrapped myself in the blanket from my bed,
and headed down to the bar in my slippers.
I had no optimism for finding shoes,
optimism or shoes I did not choose to lose,
but is not that always the way some days.
Some days and some ways,
are better than others,
and sometimes slippers fit better,
than shoes.

"A drink, a drink, I am! I am, in need!"
I cried as I slammed open the door,
with less haste and more speed.
"Take a seat" said the barman
and he pointed to a stool between,
the Sailor and the Doctor,
between one man,
and another.

"Wine please, any wine will do."

"Red or white?"
"Wine please, any wine will do."

He set before me a large glass,
and filled it to the brim,
with wine gums black, red, green and yellow
all the colours of my sorrow and tomorrow.
I opened my mouth to complain but in his eyes I saw the pain,
black, red, green and yellow,
my sorrow and his tomorrow.
The gums stuck in my throat and I never took a bite,
yet I drank and ate my fill that night.

"This is poetry" he said.
"What is?"
"What you just said."
I turned and looked to the doctor,
and he looked at me and said,
"I've got one for you."
"One what?"
"Just listen"
"Ok" I said, I had no choice over the slippers and shoes
neither gums nor booze.

"The eyes of dead men are black, green, red or yellow.
The world spins from yesterday to tomorrow.
Slabs of meat walking on two feet
are all some men,
are.
Stop, wait, go, stop, wait, go,
they never get very far.
And even if you are of body able,
you will still end up as meat on my table."

I turned to the Sailor and asked
"How is life at sea?"
"Life at sea is a lot like crossing this space between you and me.
Up and down with a smile or frown,
sometimes you need a moment to think,

or a moment to drink.
The sea and the space are always there to cross,
sail or no the wind and the tide care not,
and solid ground is all too often forgot."

I turned back to the barman.
"Next time I really would enjoy a glass of wine."
"You can drink when you are old enough,
when you have had enough and seen enough,
and know enough to fill a glass with things less sweet."

"I'm a writer" I said "look here is my desk and space,
and this,
this is my face."
They all looked me square in the eye,
as the barman dealt his reply,
"you'll be of drinking age when you can fill that blank page."
And that was all he had to say on that day,
And I had nothing else to say that day.

I left my blanket and security at the bar,
as my slippers carried my feet and my confusion.
It was still cold outside,
and the rain began to pour,
from my eyes to my lips.
At last,
at long lonely last,
I had something to drink.

Bound To Be

It is too dark to see so I close my eyes.
Ahead I can make out the shape of a wooden ladder,
beyond the blackness, stained with purples and blues.
My eyes have been open for far too long.
As I creep forward,
each creak of the floor,
ratchets the names and more,
of those I had forgotten, feelings forsaken.

Each ring of the ladder,
approaches with an exhalation,
as gravity makes a proclamation.
A catch of the breath,
between each step is all,
I have ever known,
the only way I have grown.

My head leans into a ceiling with a tease,
there is an attempt at resistance,
but then something gives,
as it always does.
And with a grasp of a breeze and a gasp of a draught,
I ascend through a trap,
door.

This darkness is fresh,
a fashioned firmament, figurative and foreboding.
Feelings flutter finding fears,
as another aspect appears.
 I open my eyes and black melts to grey,
there is an implication of candlelight,
its source ambiguous in my plight.

There are shapes. Forms, bodies,
suspended from the ceiling.

Their hair that dangles tickles the floor with each step,
with each beat I find them bound,
eyes closed and in state.

There is a woman to my right,
she sways ever so slightly
as her mass seeks the draught I create.
Her curves call to me,
bursting and bound,
in rope and emotion.
A desire revels in the darkness
and the absence of light.
I reach out to touch her breast,
bursting and bound,
bulging and bound.

As I touch her I am struck,
by a shock and a sound,
a charge of static knocks me to the ground.
All of the bodies let out a scream
as their eyes remain closed,
their limbs bound in throws.
A light appears ahead,
from a door that is no longer,
closed.

I cannot make out the room ahead for the light,
but in the white rectangle
from right angle to each angle
a woman is suspended,
upside down and all around
neither bound or apprehended.
Her hair also strokes the floor and her legs
keep her body pressed to the door frame
as her face turns towards me.
She says nothing
and looks at nothing.

With grace and pace
she sets herself upright,
like the twist of a sand timer.
I freeze before her,
I stand in awe of her.
I find definitions in her thighs
and metaphors in her eyes.

I desire her,
I open my mouth to breath her,
but there is a paralysis of words.
Guilt and shame are my girth.

"Look you did. Touch you did. Ask you did not."
In her voice I hear every name and every twist and creak,
from every step and beat I took across the floor.
The sound is silence and screams in violence.
"Look you did. Touch you did. Ask you did not."

A coiling, a boiling, emits from the floor.
Neither a snake nor serpent but a cord,
cold with compulsion,
probing with percussion
that now wraps around my feet.
It squeezes and wrangles,
pounds and strangles,
every inch of my being,
every pound of my flesh.

I groan in ecstasy and catch fire in desire,
until there is no air in my lungs
and no fluid in my loins.
And with twist and a gist I too
am suspended from the ceiling,
devoid of all feeling.

My eyes stare wide open,
at the door now closed
my pupils dilated and vacated.

I cannot make a sound,
there are no feelings to be found.
In darkness I am suspended,
with no defense of blindless,
as my heart beats a call to be bound tighter,
until this cord dissects my being.
Who knows how long I will dangle from the ceiling,
but in darkness devoid of feeling,
time is bereft of meaning.

The dead air, suffocates.
I thirst for a breeze.

Fuck Me

Fuck me.
I'm bored.
Every day is the same
and every face is the same.
These people bear no name,
ragtags of hashtags and leather bags
they think they want
but never want to think
about what,
they want.
I want.
To think.
About somebody, anybody and not nobody,
for a change.

Fuck me.
She said.
Fuck me I'm bored.
Make my toes curl harder than your little fella,
and my body shake until I sing a cappella.

Fuck me.
I said.
You need to climb on top until you come,
and I have to hang on and hang on until you're done.

Fuck me.
I'm bored.
I'm daydreaming again.
My rotator cuff with a huff
has stopped me writing,
stopped me wanking,
and the woman who wants to get fucked has no name.
Every day is the fucking same.
We want everybody to fuck off,
but we want to get fucked,
all the same.
Fuck off.

Fuck me.
Fuck me in the ear.
Fuck me in the eye.
Fuck me in the ass.
Fuck me until I die.
Fuck me in school.
Fuck me for not being cool.
Fuck me for breaking the rules.
Fuck me for thinking.
Fuck me for drinking.
Fuck me for being.
Fuck me.
I'm sinking.

Fuck me.
I'm bored.

Fuck.

I could go for a walk,
but it's so cold the air is clinging to the windows to get warm.
Fuck.
I can't see shit outside except the cold outside,
and the ash spilt on the floor,
and I forgot my slippers.
Fuck this floor.
Fuck this metaphor.

Fuck me.
I'm bored.

FUCK.

Acid

Wanting.
More.
To be next to you,
in my own skin,
is not close enough,
not deep enough.
To be the ink,
in your tattoo,
injected deep into,
a part of you,
could be something,
I guess.
Or perhaps,
the acid in your stomach,
to drown every,
single lump,
you throw down your mouth.
To dissolve,
every piece of a lie,
that you think is good enough,
to swallow,
could be something,
I guess.
But would it be enough?
That skin will stretch,
and wrinkle,
and sag.
That stomach,
will stretch,
and wrinkle,
and bag.
And I,
am just a man,
who like many others,
thinks he has fallen in love,
but really just wants to be inside you,
for a moment.
To feel a moment,

The hopeless desire to meld into and become one with the other. Impossible: it pisses me off such feelings exist

Nonchalance of he that no longer has hope of attaining these goals.

real sense of bitterness: in this journey to meld, we become bitter because it doesn't exist.

Never and then...

decay

148

live in a moment,
until that moment,
is the past.
Until that moment,
is our last,
because such a moment is not long enough,
and we rarely do really love,
another,
enough.
The flaw in the idea of love,
is that it is a notion,
a mutual commotion,
but the action,
we perform,
alone.
The idea of somebody,
is all too often,
our own.

[Handwritten annotations:]

This moment of orgasmic ecstasy is it experienced mindfully, the apex of human experience; and yet we have smothered this purity with

BS pressures:
'love'
'marriage'

— why can't we accept what we are and stay in the moment?

Profoundly heartbreaking

Do we ever love another, truly?

Can we ever love someone else taking into account we will never FULLY know who they are.

Do we not love just the idea of this person — a manufactured, prefabricated construct of 'my partner' —

— and on this manufactured construct we lay all the weight of our hope and fear — which is an unbearable ask of any soul.

Blood On The Snow

This is my favourite weather, crisp, dry winter sun and freshly powdered snow. It crunches under my feet like velvet and sounds like the chomp of crisps. My breath, mist, meanders from my mouth. I am surprised that it does not reach very far in front of me, before it vanishes. I wonder if the last breath we breathe will look the same as the rest, will it reach further than the others, in one last desperate reach for beyond? I wonder. I ponder, upon many things, as many as the snowflakes that lay the blanket I tread upon, above which I now dream upon.

All is quiet, no whisper of a breeze, no bird song in the trees, the only noise to find is that of the thoughts in my mind and my feet upon snow. I begin to head up the hill that leads to the woods beyond and my breaths become shorter and faster. At the top of the hill, I look back to see the house I left. All my days I have lived there and all my nights I have slept there, under that roof under the sky that grants the gift of snow, and the sun that will again make the flowers grow.

I turn back around, and a contrast becomes my new path, there are marks on the ground. A near black on the near white and the world for a moment, is monochromatic, a hued dramatic. I stoop down like a raven and touch the spots on the ground. There is blood on the snow, as fresh as the sun and the air around me, and as rich as the thoughts that make me.

I look up and see more ahead, leading off towards the forest and I began to follow, my steps beating a rhythm of sorrow. What manner of man or beast, has bled upon the snow? I wonder. I ponder upon this and many things as my heart sings in fear, as more blood draws, near.

I recall playing in the garden in the house as I child. My first winter and snowballs in my hands. My first wet dream under the blankets and my mind imagining life beyond the hills and the woods. Days, years, wondering, pondering, about life beyond the hills and woods.

Eventually the tracks lead me to the edge of the woods, and I encounter some resistance. I have to peel back branches and twigs, leaves and thorns to move beyond. My eyes squint and my hands are scratched but I still make out blood upon the path. Eventually before me, the trail ends at the foot of a great tree. The roots are wild and broad and covered with all manner of moss, ivies and blood. Deep, black, red blood. In frustration and desperation I attack the roots with my hands, tear apart the ivies and burrow and furrow until a light appears under the bloodstained earth and twigs.

My hands touch a coldness beyond the snow, there is glass here, a mirror at the base of the tree at the end of this bloody path. At the end of this bloody path, I find my reflection. I gaze upon my face for the first time in my life and know then, that there is so much more to see in this world.

https://www.instagram.com/juxtaproser/